FLY GUY AND THE ALIENZZ

Tedd Arnold

Cartwheel Books

An Imprint of Scholastic Inc.

For Alexandra, Raegan, Cole, and Mason — a team of real Secret Heroes!

All rights reserved. Published by Scholastic Inc., *Publishers since 1920.* SCHOLASTIC, CARTWHEEL BOOKS, and associated logos are trademarks and/or registered trademarks of Scholastic Inc.

Library of Congress Cataloging-in-Publication Data available

ISBN 978-0-545-66318-2

10 9 8 7 6 5 4 3 2 1   18 19 20 21 22

Printed in China 38

First edition, May 2018

Book design by Kirk Benshoff

A boy had a pet fly.
He named him Fly Guy.
Fly Guy could say
the boy's name —

Chapter 1

One day, Buzz said, "Hey, Fly Guy, I'm making a movie!"

FUNZZIE!

"It will be about aliens," said Buzz.

"Aliens are guys that come from space," said Buzz.

"No, silly," said Buzz. "They look like this. I drew them, cut them out, and glued them on sticks, like puppets."

"This is you and me," said Buzz.
"And I made us a cool fort."

"And here's an alien riding on his awesome solid-gold spaceship."

Buzz set up the camera and said, "Quiet on the set. And ACTION!" Then he started telling a story.

Scene 1

"One day, in the future," said Buzz, "Fly Guy and Buzz Boy were flying around."

"They were guarding the Secret Hero Fort."

"An alien spaceship snuck up behind Fly Guy and Buzz Boy."

"The aliens turned on their ray beam. The ray beam pulled the heroes into the spaceship."

"Inside the spaceship, all the aliens jumped on top of Buzz Boy. They tied him up."

Scene 2

"Fly Guy flew back to the Secret Hero Fort to get help."

"Their pal, Dragon Dude, came out and shot fireballs at the spaceship."

"The solid-gold spaceship was fireproof. But the fireballs made the aliens mad. They crushed the Secret Hero Fort."

"Fly Guy was trapped inside the Secret Hero Fort."

"The aliens jumped on top of Dragon Dude. They tried to tie him up, but it was not easy!"

Scene 3

"Suddenly, Fly Girl arrived!"

"The aliens were busy with Dragon Dude. They didn't see her rescue Fly Guy from the Secret Hero Fort."

"Fly Guy and Fly Girl flew around the aliens very fast."

"The aliens shot at them
with fly-swatter shooters."

"They missed and hit each
other instead."

"When no one was looking, space pirates came and stole the solid-gold spaceship."

"They took it back to their creepy pirate planet."

"Without a ship, the aliens were stuck on Earth. They surrendered and joined the Secret Hero team."

"Fly Guy and Fly Girl and all the Secret Heroes protected Earth happily ever after."

"The end," said Buzz.

"Oops!" said Buzz, "Buzz Boy is still tied up on the solid-gold spaceship that the pirates took!"

"Good thing you thought of that, Fly Guy! We need to make a movie sequel. We must rescue Buzz Boy."

"Okay," said Buzz, "quiet on the set. And ACTION!"